Not the Piano, Mrs. Medley!

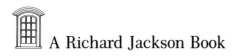 A Richard Jackson Book

Story by EVAN LEVINE
Pictures by S. D. SCHINDLER

Orchard Books   New York

Not the Piano, Mrs. Medley!

Orchard Books, A division of Franklin Watts, Inc., 387 Park Avenue South, New York, NY 10016

Manufactured in the United States of America. Printed by General Offset Company, Inc. Bound by
Horowitz/Rae. Book design by Mina Greenstein

The text of this book is set in 14 point Primer. The illustrations are watercolor and gouache,
reproduced in full color.   10   9   8   7   6   5   4   3   2   1

Library of Congress Cataloging-in-Publication Data
Levine, Evan. Not the piano, Mrs. Medley! / story by Evan Levine ; pictures by S. D.
Schindler.   p.   cm. "A Richard Jackson book."   Summary: After several false starts, Mrs. Medley,
loaded with gear, sets out for the beach with her grandson Max and her dog Word.
ISBN 0-531-05956-1.   ISBN 0-531-08556-2 (lib. bdg.)
[1. Beaches—Fiction.   2. Grandmothers—Fiction.]   I. Schindler, S. D., ill.
II. Title.   PZ7.L57834No   1991   [E]—dc20   90-29085

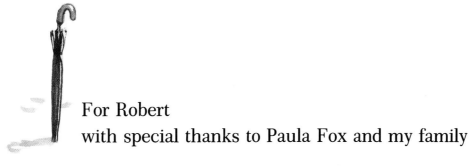

For Robert
with special thanks to Paula Fox and my family

—E.L.

O N THURSDAY, Mrs. Medley decided to go to the beach.
She had just moved into a new house and hadn't seen the sea yet.
   "Come, Max," she said to her grandson, who was visiting her.
   "Come, Word," she said to her dog. "Let's go to the beach.
We will need some towels."
   Mrs. Medley took out a big blue towel for herself, a
medium blue towel for Max, and a little blue towel for Word.

They were all the way down the block when Mrs. Medley stopped.

"Even though the sun is shining now, it might rain later," she said. "Let's go back and get some rain things."

"It doesn't look like rain, Grandma," said Max. "Let's get to the beach."

"Well, you never know," said Mrs. Medley.

So Mrs. Medley and Max and Word walked back home.

"I think Word will be fine," Mrs. Medley said. "But *we* need raincoats and an umbrella, just in case." She also packed hats and sweaters and boots.

"Boots, Grandma?" said Max.

"Well, if it doesn't rain, they are very good for catching sand crabs," said Mrs. Medley.

"Why do you want to catch sand crabs?" asked Max.

"Oh, you never know when you might suddenly need some sand crabs," said Mrs. Medley.

They were all the way down two blocks when Mrs. Medley stopped.

"Oh, dear, I didn't bring any toys," she said.

"We don't need toys," said Max. "We can bury our toes with sand and make monsters out of clamshells. Let's get to the beach."

"But we might want other things," said Mrs. Medley.

So she and Max and Word walked back home.

Mrs. Medley took out a bucket and a shovel and a Monopoly set.

"Won't it be hard to play Monopoly on the sand?" asked Max.

"You're right," said Mrs. Medley. "We'll bring a table."

"Grandma, a table at the beach?" asked Max.

"Well," said Mrs. Medley. "We can't play Monopoly without it."

"I don't even like Monopoly," said Max. But Mrs. Medley was busy trying to fit a table in a bag.

"We need chairs," she said. "Maybe the ones from the kitchen."

"Chairs?" said Max. "At the beach?"

"Yes," said Mrs. Medley. "It will be more comfortable when we play Monopoly. Especially if we bring pillows."

She brought out two chairs. "I have an idea," she said.

She tied the chairs on a skateboard.

"We seem to have an awful lot," said Max. "Do we really need all this?"

Mrs. Medley looked surprised. "Of course," she said.

"Are you sure there's nothing else we need, Grandma?" asked Max.

"Of course not," said Mrs. Medley. "What else could we need?"

"I don't know, Grandma," said Max. "I just want to get to the beach."

"Going to a yard sale?" a neighbor yelled, as they left.

"How silly," said Mrs. Medley. "We're going to the beach. Can't everyone tell?"

They walked down the block and turned the corner.

Things fell. Word panted. Max sighed.

When they were all the way down three blocks, they could see the bright sea shining and bouncing in the sun, like a million new blue balloons rolling. Suddenly Mrs. Medley stopped.

"Oh, no," said Max. Word looked disappointed.

"I just thought," said Mrs. Medley, "that we might want music."

"We don't *need* music," said Max. "Let's get to the beach!"

"But you might change your mind," said Mrs. Medley.

So Mrs. Medley and Max and Word crossed the street, turned the corner, and walked home.

Feet dragged. Chairs bumped. Word whined.

"We'll *never* get to the beach," Max said grumpily.

Mrs. Medley found a radio, extra batteries, a tape deck, and cassettes.

"Maybe we should also take the record player," she said.

"Grandma, we can't possibly USE all this stuff," said Max.

"Well, we might get tired of one thing and then want something else," said Mrs. Medley. "But we will need another bag. And as long as we are taking another one, we can take the xylophone, the recorder, and the bongo drums!"

"Grandma, can you play the bongo drums?" asked Max.

"No," said Mrs. Medley. "But this might be a good afternoon to learn. Perhaps you should take the accordion so you can accompany me! We will also bring a bell for Word. And we will need a music stand and a conductor's baton!"

"Oh, dear," she said. "They won't all fit in the bag." She put everything in a red wagon.

"Are you *sure* we need all this stuff, Grandma?" asked Max. "We will *never* get to the beach!"

"Oh, yes," said Mrs. Medley. "It's important to be prepared."

They were all the way down four blocks when Mrs. Medley said, "What about . . ."

"No!" said Max. *"No No No No No! LET'S JUST GET TO THE BEACH!"*

Word looked relieved.

"Oh, all right," said Mrs. Medley. "I'm sure that we will be the best prepared people there, anyway."

They moved slowly across the sand. Suddenly Mrs. Medley stopped.

"Uh, oh," said Max.

"Look at that," said Mrs. Medley.

"What?" said Max. "Is it someone with more chairs? A bedroom set? Everything in his refrigerator?"

"It's the sea," said Mrs. Medley. "It's so big and so blue and
so . . . wet!"

Word galloped to the edge of the waves.

"Look at that," Mrs. Medley said. "Word is having a good time,
isn't he? Let's go look."

"Don't you want to set up the table and chairs?" Max asked.

"Well, no, not quite yet," she said.

Mrs. Medley stared out across the sea.

"My, how big it is!" she exclaimed. "There is a sailboat! And there are some sea gulls! And I bet there are clams! Let's start digging and see if we can find some!"

"What about Monopoly, Grandma?" asked Max.

"Monopoly?" said Mrs. Medley. "We can play Monopoly at home. Now that we're at the beach, we should do beach things. Let's run along the shore! Let's play beach volleyball!"

"Don't you want to put on your rain boots, Grandma?" asked Max.

"What for?" said Mrs. Medley. "The water feels so nice and cool."

"What about the bongo drums and the xylophone?" asked Max.

"They won't feel as good on my feet as the water," said Mrs. Medley.

"I meant to play," said Max.

"If we play with those, we won't be able to hear the waves," said Mrs. Medley.

"Grandma," said Max. "We don't really need any of that stuff. We don't need bongo drums or raincoats or Monopoly sets. We just need . . ." He stopped. "*Grandma*," said Max, "we forgot our *bathing suits*!"

"Bathing suits?" said Mrs. Medley. "Mercy, so we did!"
She looked at Max, and they began to laugh.
"Perhaps I packed just a little bit too much," she said.

"It's all right, Grandma," said Max. "At least we are here! Let's put our feet in the water and build sand castles."

"Let's do that," said Mrs. Medley. "And tomorrow, when we go to the park, I won't take as much stuff."

"I know, Grandma," said Max, giving her a hug. "All we will need is a globe and a badminton set and an ice cream maker and a garbage disposal and a piano . . ."

"A piano?" said Mrs. Medley. "Oh, Max, you're so silly!"